The Astounding Adventure of

Mr Bowns

(the Laziest Man in the World)

Ade Bowen

To Josh

Don't be ?
Lazy Bo~

Onion Custard Kids

The Astounding Adventure of Mr Bowns
The Laziest Man in the World
Astounding Adventures: Book 1

British Library Cataloguing in Publication Data.
A catalogue record for this book is available from the British
Library.

Published in the United Kingdom by Onion Custard Kids,
an imprint of Wordcatcher Publishing Group Ltd
www.wordcatcher.com
Tel: 02921 888321
Facebook.com/WordcatcherPublishing

First Edition: 2019
Print edition ISBN: 9781911265856
Ebook edition ISBN: 9781911265498

Category: Children's 5-8 years

I would like to thank:
my daughters, Willow and Phoebe,
for listening to my stories;
my parents, Lyn and John,
for always believing in me;
and my wife Rosie
for tidying up after me.

Much of this story was written while I was
backpacking around Germany. I want to give a special
thanks to the German student who kindly let me stay
with him when I couldn't afford a hotel.
His name has been lost over time,
but his generosity has never been forgotten.

Contents

One

Mr Bowns looked at the witch staring at him across the dusty old room. He was standing in the middle of a ring of fire and the witch was pointing her bony finger straight at him, ready to cast a nasty spell.

His friends were unable to help, and he couldn't think of a single thing he could do to stop her.

His mind went back to that morning. *I should have never got out of bed!* he thought to himself.

Well, we can all relate to that.

Confused?

OK, let's go back in time, and I'll tell you the story of how Mr Bowns, the laziest man in the world, got into this mess.

Two

This is the story of a very lazy man called Mr Bowns. Mr Bowns is really lazy. Really, really lazy. Really, really, really lazy. Mr Bowns is the laziest man ever. You may think you are lazy because you don't want to tidy your bedroom once a month, but that has nothing on him. He could get a degree in being lazy, if he could be bothered sitting the exam, or going to university. Or getting out of bed!

He is so lazy he doesn't even turn over in his sleep!

He is so lazy he doesn't sneeze, because sneezing would take too much effort. If he did sneeze, he wouldn't bother moving for the rest of the month.

Lazy Mr Bowns!

Mr Bowns lives in a town called Quicksnap. Quicksnap is a small village where people farm popcorn from popcorn trees. They squeeze gorgeous, fizzy lemonade straight out of fresh lemons. And they grow the gooiest chocolate cake straight out of the ground. What? You didn't know that chocolate cake grows out of the ground? It doesn't just turn up on the shelves of your local supermarket by magic you know!

Everybody in the village was happy with their life and whistled as they worked through the day under the friendly sun.

In the evening they would go down to the Open Arms Tavern and share stories, tell jokes and laugh the night away.

Everybody that was, except Mr Bowns, because he was too lazy. He doesn't even poo! That's how lazy Mr Bowns is!

No, Mr Bowns didn't go to the Tavern with the other village folk – it was too much effort. Mr Bowns didn't help out in the fields picking popcorn, squeezing lemonade of harvesting gooey chocolate cake because that was far too early in the morning.

Mr Bowns didn't even have hair on the top of his head because growing hair would be far too taxing.

"Effort, effort effort!" he would always say, then turn over and go back to sleep.

Poor old lazy Bowns, what was he missing out on?

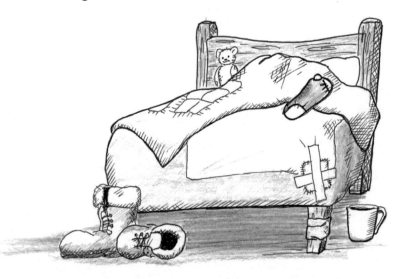

However, Mr Bowns did have a wonderful imagination. While he sat in bed doing nothing, just looking at the four walls, he would think of the most amazing stories, poems and riddles. And he would tell them to Joanna and Jake, the children who lived next door.

Every day Joanna and Jake would be sent by their mother to Mr Bowns' house to help him out. As they worked, he would entertain them with songs and stories of magic and dragons and brave knights and castles in faraway lands.

The children would dress up and pretend to be the characters in the stories as they helped with the chores. Soon the house would be spick and span. Not that there was ever much mess. You might think that with Mr Bowns being so lazy, his house would be filthy and dirty – but no.

He was so lazy, he couldn't be bothered to make a mess!

Three

Our story really starts one exceptionally fine summer's afternoon when Mr Bowns decided to get up. It was such a sunny day that he thought for once it would be a good day for a walk.

So, when he could be bothered, he got dressed.

When he recovered from that, he put his shoes on.

And when he felt like it, he opened the door and went outside.

"Good afternoon, Mr Bowns," said Jake and Joanne, who were playing outside.

"Good afternoon children," said Mr Bowns, his kind old eyes sparkling in the sunlight. "Could you be so kind as to open my gate for me?"

"Certainly," answered Joanne. "Where are you going?"

"I'm going for a walk."

"Can we come with you and listen to another story please?" asked Jake.

"Yes, please!" squealed Joanna. "Where are we going?"

Mr Bowns stopped in his tracks. Where *was* he going? He hadn't thought about that. He looked left. He looked right. He looked left again. It had been so long since he'd gone out, he couldn't think of anywhere to go.

"I think we should go left. It's all downhill that way."

Typical Mr Bowns!

So, off they went.

The children told Mr Bowns about their day and the latest news from the village. Mr Bowns made up stories, and they all sang songs to pass the time. Their favourite was the Friendship Song, and it they sang it long and loud:

With friends like these, with friends like these.

When you get in trouble, I'll be there on the double.

I'll be there for you, I will always pull you through.

With friends like these.

If you're feeling down, I will act just like a clown

Just to make you smile, I'll be there all the while

If you ever get stuck, do not worry, you're in luck

With friends like these.

Each time they came to a junction, Mr Bowns would choose the path to take. The more they talked and sang, the more they walked, and the more they walked, the deeper they went into the wood. Down they went, following the road, until they could no longer see Quicksnap, and the trees got thicker and more twisted and strange animals looked at them from the undergrowth.

One animal looked like a cross between a poodle and crocodile. They called it a crocopoo, and they all laughed.

If this was you, would you have taken note of the way you came so you could find your way back? That would have been a good idea, but because they were having such a good time, they didn't realise how far into the valley they had gone until the road stopped at a gate.

Mr Bowns halted mid-story and looked at the gate. They looked at each other. Finally, they looked all around them.

They could just about see the sun peeking through the thick and twisted trees and bushes. Weird shadows crept out of the darkness and reached towards them. The wind whistled, making an eerie howling noise that sent shivers down their spines. Spooky!

Beyond the gate was a path leading to a rundown cottage. They would have thought it deserted if it weren't for a single, lit candle in one window.

All three were very scared. They didn't know where they were, how they had got there, or how they were going to get home. It would be dark soon and the strange noises of the forest around them were unsettling.

What worried them most was the cottage in front of them. It would soon be night, and one of them was going to have to ask for directions. Something about the cottage didn't feel right. It was like a dragon waiting to pounce. The house looked alive and angry, and none of them wanted to go nearer.

Four

"I think you should go," said Joanna to Jake. "You are always so polite and courteous. You should ask."

Jake immediately stuck his fingers up his nose and said, "Me? Polite? I don't think so, Pig Nose! I think Mr Bowns should go. He's so knowledgeable. He'll know what to do."

"Erm, good point young Jake, but I'm too lazy to walk all the way down there," yawned Mr Bowns.

And so the discussion went on and on, with them trying to convince each other who should be the one to approach the cottage.

"This is no good," said Mr Bowns after a while. "We will have to draw sticks to decide."

So, Joanna found three sticks – two long and one short. Hiding the length of each stick, she held the tops of them up for the others to choose.

They took it in turns to pick a stick. Jake went first and he picked a long stick and drew a big sigh of relief.

Then Mr. Bowns chose. His was the second long stick, and he drew a little sigh of relief because he couldn't muster the strength to give a big one.

With just the short stick left, Joanna slowly opened the gate and crept up the long, overgrown path. She shook with fear every step of the way.

She knocked on the cottage door.

BOOM! BOOM! BOOM!

The sound echoed through the forest and they heard movement from the trees. Minutes ticked by. Just as Joanna was about to give up, the door opened a tiny crack.

CREAK!

Joanna said in a trembling voice, "Hello. My name is Joanna and I'm awfully lost. Which is the way back to Quicksnap please?"

The door open wider, and Joanna walked into the darkness of the cottage.

Nothing happened. The sun sank behind the trees, the shadows got longer and it was dark.

Jake and Mr Bowns began to worry.

"One of us really should go in and make sure Joanna is OK," said Mr Bowns.

"Yes, you should go because you are older and they will listen to you," Jake replied.

"No, no, no. You should go because you are friendlier than I am, and they will give you what you need."

Again, they argued, as the sun disappeared.

"This is no good. Let's play rock, paper, scissors to decide. Best of three."

Jake agreed and he won the first round with his paper wrapping the stone. Mr Bowns won the second round when his scissors beat Jake's paper.

It was all down to the third round, and Mr Bowns pulled a stone to Jake's scissors.

Stone blunts scissors, so Mr Bowns won, and it was Jake with trembling legs that walked up the path and knocked on the cottage door.

After a while, the door creaked open again.

CREAK!

Mr Bowns heard Jake say "H h h h h hello. I'm looking for my sister. She came in asking for directions to Quicksnap. Can you help me?"

He watched as the door opened wider and Jake also went into the cottage.

Nothing happened.

Everything was dark, apart from the flickering candlelight in the window.

Five

As Mr Bowns waited and waited for the children to come out of the spooky cottage, he thought, *This isn't good. This is not good at all! I'm going to have to go and ask for directions myself. Oh, effort, effort, effort!*

With that, he made his way up the path. He was about to knock on the door, when he thought twice about it and walked to the window instead.

Carefully, he looked in through the dirty glass and at a scene that made his

toes curl. There, in the middle of the
room was the biggest cooking pot he had
ever seen. The pot rested on a log fire
and inside it were his friends, Joanna and
Jake!

In the room was another figure, dressed in a purple cloak with its back to the window. Mr Bowns knew that if he was to save the children, he would have to act fast. Well fast-ish. Well as fast as he could. Well, he would have to do something, but fast? Let's not be too hasty.

He said to himself, "Oh, such effort! I'll have to think. Now, if this is a big old cottage in the deepest, darkest part of the forest valley, and my friends have been kidnapped and put in a big old cooking pot, that can only mean... Oh my! This must be a witch's cottage. Oh dearie, dearie me. I knew I shouldn't have moved today. Effort always gets you into trouble."

But Mr Bowns knew that he had to rescue his friends. It was his idea to go for a walk and he really should have been the first to ask for directions.

So, he snuck around the back of the cottage where he found the back door open. He cautiously looked inside.

On the floor in front of a broomstick was a big ginger cat with one eye open looking out the door.

Luckily, Mr Bowns saw the cat first and moved out of sight before he was noticed.

"How am I going to get past that cat?" Mr Bowns said quietly to himself. "If this is a witch's cottage, that cat is bound to be magic. If he sees me, he will tell the witch. Then, who will save the children?"

"Who indeed!" said a gravelly voice from behind him, and if Mr Bowns wasn't so lazy, he would have jumped out of his skin in fright. Turning slowly, he looked to see where the voice had come from. He couldn't see anything, other than an old bucket next to the run-down back wall of the cottage.

"Did you say something, bucket?"

"What a dope! He thinks a bucket can talk!" answered the voice.

"Shush, not so loud," Mr Bowns whispered. "Who are you then?"

"I'm the cottage wall, silly," said the cottage wall.

"Oh, silly me, thinking it was a bucket talking and not a wall. Do you know walls don't talk either?"

"I do. Being the wall of a witch's cottage, some of her magic has seeped into me and now I can talk."

Suddenly, Mr Bowns was worried. "You're not going to tell the witch about me, are you?" he asked, slowly edging away from the wall, getting ready to walk away if there was any trouble (he would run, but that would be too much effort).

"No, I'll help you rescue your friends... if you help me."

"How can I help you? You're a wall."

"Well I use to be a lovely cottage. I had nice white paint on my walls, shiny clear windows, and I used to be all warm and cosy. But the witch doesn't look after me. My paint is falling off and my windows are dirty. I am messy inside and the big

holes in my roof
let in the wind and rain.
I'm quite lonely."

Mr Bowns looked at the cottage.
It did look horrible. Old plaster had fallen
off to expose the brickwork underneath.
All that remained of the white paint was
dirty grey flakes on a bare brick wall. And
cobwebs were hanging everywhere.

Weeds from the garden crept all over
it. Mr Bowns felt quite sorry for the wall.
Then, to his surprise, the wall started to
cry. Huge plops of water fell through the
windows, the walls shook, tiles fell from
the roof and it made terrible sobbing
noises.

"Shush there, don't cry," Mr Bowns
comforted the wall. "Please don't cry,
you'll bring the witch over. I'll help you
after I've rescued my friends, Jake and
Joanna. We will all make sure you get
looked after."

"Promise?" the wall asked, sniffing back its tears.

"I promise. Now, how do I get past that cat?" asked Mr Bowns, turning his attention back to the door.

"Oh, that's easy... pretend to be a mouse!"

Six

Mr Bowns thought about the idea of pretending to be a mouse to fool the cat. The idea appealed to his sense of imagination (and his sense of laziness), so he decided it could work.

He crouched next to the door. Clearing his throat, and in a high squeaky voice, he said, "There's that big fat cat again. He is so slow he couldn't catch a cold. And he is stupid. I bet he couldn't find a mouse in his paws if we gave him a map."

Mr Bowns paused to look through a gap in the door and, sure enough, the cat was standing up and looking angry.

In a slightly different squeaky-mouse voice, he continued, "Have you ever smelt the old, fat cat? He is so smelly! I thought cats looked after themselves, but this one couldn't look after his own shadow. He must be the scruffiest, smelliest, stupidest, slowest, fattest cat ever! We can stay here all night and he couldn't do anything about it."

The cat didn't like that at all! He ran out the door as fast as his fat legs could carry him, across the garden, through a bush and out into the woods to find his tormentors.

"That was clever!" said the cottage wall. Now go inside and save your friends. The water in the pot will soon start to boil, but you need to be careful of the broomstick."

"OK, thanks," replied Mr Bowns. He got up and walked through the door into the kitchen. Dirty pots and pans lay around the place and broken cupboards lay empty. As Mr Bowns crept towards the closed door, something stirred in the corner of the room. He turned and saw the witch's broomstick march between him and the door.

"Halt, who goes there?" demanded the broomstick in its best bossy Sergeant Major voice.

"Um, Mr Bowns, sir," answered Mr Bowns before he could stop himself. He had hoped to sneak past the broomstick before it noticed him. It would have been much less effort.

"What is your business, Mr Bowns?" asked the broomstick.

"I don't know," Mr Bowns answered, and under his breath, he whispered, "Wall, how do I get out of this one?"

"It is a proud and loyal broomstick. You have to trick it," replied the wall.

"But how?" If Mr Bowns could be bothered, he'd be worried.

"Well if you don't know, you'll have to go," answered the wall.

"No, I need to get through that door." Mr Bowns surprised himself. Normally the only thing that Mr Bowns needed was to stay in bed, but the children being in trouble had stirred something in him. It was

a   strange sensation he had

not felt before. He *wanted* to help his friends. He *needed* to help his friends.

"Well you can't go through the door," said the broomstick. "There is no way you could outsmart me. I'm the best at everything I do!"

Slowly, an idea formed in Mr Bowns' head, one that didn't require too much effort, so he liked it.

"So, you think you are the best at everything do you?"

"I don't think so, I know so."

"OK, so if I beat you at something, will you let me in?"

"Ha, if you beat me at anything, not only will I allow you through the door, but I will give you a lift home. That's how confident I am. You can challenge me to three tasks and if you win just one of them, you win. OK?"

"That sounds very fair indeed, thank you. My first challenge is that I bet I could tidy this room faster than you. On your marks, get set, go!"

On 'go' the broomstick turned into a blur as it raced around the room, picking up pots and pans, fixing cupboards, dusting surfaces, sweeping floors, stacking cups, and polishing taps. Mr Bowns felt quite ill. Just watching something working so hard made him feel tired and he had to sit down.

The broomstick finished and the kitchen was sparkling clean. Mr Bowns had to admit that it had done an excellent job.

"Thank you very much," said the wall. I feel a bit better already with my kitchen tidy, but aren't you worried that you're lost?"

"Don't worry, I still have two challenges."

"I won that one," said the broomstick. "Try again."

"Thank you," answered Mr Bowns. "For my next challenge, I say that I look better than you in the moonlight."

"Ha. I bet you don't," and with that, the broomstick rushed outside, followed slowly by Mr Bowns.

Outside the moon was full and shining down on them.

"Well, I think I look best. I am made of wood and the trees are made of wood, so I fit in naturally. You, however, are messy and you look out of place here. You lose. I win!"

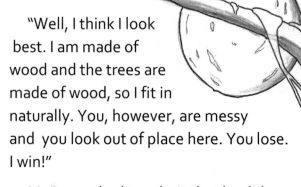

Mr Bowns had to admit that he did look a mess, but he always found it too much effort to comb his hair or iron his clothes.

"Yes, it won again. Are you sure you know what you are doing?" asked the wall.

"Yes, yes," whispered Mr Bowns under his breath. Turning back to the broomstick, he said, "Now my final task. I challenge you not to move all night."

"Easy," said the broomstick, and it lay down on the grass.

"Right, while you lie there, I'm going through the door," and, with that, he walked towards the cottage.

"Hey, you can't do that! I'm supposed to be guarding the door! Hang on, if I move, you've won, but if I let you in, the witch will turn me into tinder. Oh no, this isn't fair – I must stop you."

With that, the broomstick rushed to stop Mr Bowns entering the cottage.

"A-ha! You failed. You didn't do it. You moved, so you have to let me through the door and give me a lift home. Thank you very much, Broomstick. That will save me a lot of effort."

"Ha ha, very clever," chortled the cottage. "But now is the difficult part. Be careful with the witch. She is horrible! I won't be able to help you any further."

Seven

Thanking the wall for its help beating the broomstick, Mr Bowns walked through the kitchen and up to the closed door. Slowly, without making any noise, he opened it a little and poked his head around.

In the centre of the room was the pot with Jake and Joanne inside. The fire was burning away making wisps of steam escape from the pot. The witch was busy putting things in a pot while chanting in a horrible, croaky voice. She was tall and had arms and legs that seemed much longer than normal, making her look clumsy. Her dark purple cloak wasn't quite long enough for her and her stripy stockings only came up to her knees. She wore a witch's hat, but as we know you shouldn't wear a hat indoors, it's not polite.Each time she picked something up she would add its name to the chant.

"Eye of slug, wing of bat.

Nose of a fish, how about that?

Tongue of a boy who never said please.

Hair of a hippo, not many of these.

Toe of a monkey, rock from the sea.

A cloud's silver lining, the shell of a pea.

Sweet little freckles from a young girl.

Put them together and give it a whirl."

Mr Bowns retreated into the kitchen. What was he to do? The witch had already caught Joanna, who was faster than him, and Jake, who was stronger. He would have to use his own skills to stand a chance at freeing his friends, but what was his skill? It was being lazy, and everybody knows you couldn't beat a witch by being lazy. What else could he do? He had a good imagination, but how could he imagine a way to help?

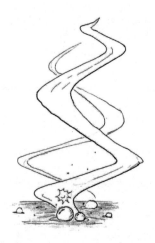

He could hear the water in the pot bubbling and if he was going to do something to save his friends, he would have to do it now. So, he took a big breath, then took another deep breath (just in case the first one was not deep enough) and stepped through the door.

Mr Bowns tried to use a big, confident voice, but it sounded more like the squeak of a mouse. He was not used to shouting – it took a lot of effort – and now his throat hurt. He hoped he wouldn't have to do that again in a hurry. He would have to lie down first. "Give back my friends," he squeaked.

Turning slowly, the witch answered in a voice that was strong and bold, much stronger than Mr Bowns expected. "No, I can't do that see, because they are going to be my tea."

'She is obviously very rude,' Mr Bowns absently thought to himself. "If you don't let them go, I'll... I'll..."

"You'll what?" asked the witch.

What could he do? He didn't know how to fight witches. He wished he was back home lying in bed. He really didn't need all of this.

"You can't beat me, whatever your plan. I'm a witch and you are a lazy old man." With that, she held up her hands, waggled her fingers and continued to chant. "To eat your friends is my desire, around your feet I will make fire."

With a boom of magic, a circle of fire appeared on the floor all around Mr Bowns, licking at his shoes and singeing his trousers. What could he do? Things looked bad. The children couldn't help him and the ring of fire was stopping him from reaching them.

Jake and Joanne saw Mr Bowns, and even though he was surrounded by fire, it enough to lift their spirits and they cheered, "Hurrah, Mr Bowns will save us!"

The children's faith in Mr Bowns gave him confidence and he thought that, with his friends belief in him, he really should be able to save them.

As he was thinking this, he noticed that the flames around him had died down. He took the opportunity and walked slowly through them and out of the circle. He would have walked quickly, but the heat was making him feel awfully tired.

He thought maybe he should have that quick lie down, but then he saw that the flames had caught his trousers on fire. He took them off and stood there in his two-week-old underpants. He looked like an ancient, wrinkly, Superman.

Now, standing in front of a witch with just your pants on is embarrassing, but doing it with two-week-old pants is *really* embarrassing. So always listen to your mum and make sure you have got clean pants on, just in case you find yourself in this position...

The witch looked alarmed at Mr Bowns' escape (and his underpants) but she didn't wait long to cast another spell. Once again she held out her hands, waggled her fingers, and said, "You escaped me once, but there is a price. Now I will turn you into ice."

Eight

Mr Bowns turned towards the children but found he couldn't. He looked down at his feet and saw that they were stuck to the floor by a block of ice that was growing up his body. He picked up a knife from the table and tried to chip his way out of it, but as soon as the knife touched the ice, it was instantly frozen solid.

The ice worked its way up his legs and halfway up his chest. The witch looked very smug and laughed at him cruelly.

"I'm best, I win, I'm magical.
You're worst, you lose, you're an icicle."

The children were terribly worried for their friend and they shouted, "Come on, Mr Bowns. You can beat it. We believe in you."

Mr Bowns heard these kind words and it gave him a warm glow in his heart. He did like having friends and he would do everything he could to rescue them. He tried to move again and found that the ice wasn't as hard now, but it would take an awful lot of effort to get out of it. And we know what old lazy Bowns thinks of effort! Still, the children cheered him on with encouraging shouts. The warm feeling in his heart spread through his body.

'I must rescue them,' he thought, and he tried to move again. To his surprise he was able to move easily. He looked down and saw that all the ice had melted. 'It must have been thawed by the warm glow of friendship I felt,' he thought. Thinking about it, the flames had gone out when the children had cheered for him. Maybe this was a clue as to how to beat the witch.

"Curses, foiled again. More magic then!" cackled the witch, and she raised her hands to cast another spell. Although he hated to do it, he had to shout again. He definitely would need a lie down after all this... probably for a whole month!

He called to his friends: "Jake, Joanne. I think I know how we can beat the witch. We have to stick together, and our friendship will beat her.

"How will that work?" asked Joanne.

"Our song!" realised Jake. "If we sing our song, we could beat her."

"Yes, let's do it!" said Joanna, and all three friends began to sing:

With friends like these, with friends like these.
When you get in trouble, I'll be there on the double.
I'll be there for you, I will always pull you through.
With friends like these.

If you're feeling down, I will act just like a clown
Just to make you smile, I'll be there all the while
If you ever get stuck, do not worry, you're in luck
With friends like these.

The witch really, really, really didn't like this, and not just because Mr Bowns was a terrible singer. Her powers were useless against friendship and love because her magic got its power from negativity.

She tried spell after spell to get them to be quiet, but no matter what she did, nothing worked. Then she started cursing them and running around the room trying to scare them, but the three friends realised that as long as they were together they were safe from her.

While the witch raced around the room, Mr Bowns helped the children out of the pot. They were wet and hot from the boiling water. They were so glad to be safe and with their friend again they hardly noticed.

They laughed and smiled at each other so much that the witch couldn't stand it anymore. She ran out of the cottage, down the garden path, up the road. She kept running long after she had disappeared from sight, chased by the crocopoo.

Mr Bowns breathed a sigh of relief as he hugged his friends. They had needed him, and with their help, he had saved them, and all without too much effort.

"Oh, thank you so much Mr Bowns for saving us," said Jake.

"It was no great effort," smiled Mr Bowns.

"But how are we going to get home?" asked Joanne.

"I have a surprise for you." Mr Bowns led them to the kitchen.

The broomstick begrudgingly let them climb onto its back, grumbling and complaining all the time.

Then flew off towards the lights of Quicksnap, far away at the top of the hill, leaving the cottage behind.

Nine

A month later, Mr Bowns was still in bed enjoying a well-deserved snooze. He was thinking about how lucky he had been during his adventure, when there was a knock at the door.

"Come in!" he called, and in came Jake and Joanne.

"Oh, hello you two. Where have you been? I haven't seen you for weeks. I thought you were upset with me because of the trouble I got you into."

"Oh, no, Mr Bowns, quite the opposite. We had such an exciting time that we have been back to the cottage to tidy it up. We thought we could use it as a base for more adventures," said Jake.

"Yes," added Joanne, "although we were scared, we didn't worry too much because we knew you were around and that you would save us."

"You have been back to that horrible place? You are brave."

"Come with us and we will show you what we have done," they said together.

After plenty of nagging and dragging, they got Mr Bowns dressed, fed, and down to the cottage.

When they arrived, Mr Bowns could not believe his eyes! There in front of him was the smartest, shiniest, prettiest looking cottage he had ever seen. The windows were fixed and gleaming, the roof had been re-thatched, the walls had been washed and re-painted and the garden pruned and mowed.

The inside had a similar transformation, the cobwebs were cleared away, the walls fixed and painted, and the old furniture replaced with beautiful handcrafted items from Quicksnap Carpenters.

"This is amazing!" Mr Bowns exclaimed. "How did you do all of this?"

Jake replied "Well, we had a bit of help." On cue, all the villagers jumped out from their hiding places and shouted "Surprise!"

Well, if Mr Bowns was not so lazy, he would have jumped out of his boots. Everybody was there, and they had brought a party with them. There was popcorn and sausages and fresh sticky chocolate cakes, all washed down with lemonade squeezed from the lemonade trees that morning.

Some of the villagers had brought their instruments and they were playing and singing. Everybody was soon dancing. Even Mr Bowns did a slow jig before finding an excuse to creep off into the kitchen for more lemonade.

Mr Bowns sat in the relative quiet of the kitchen. He breathed out a heavy sign and thought to himself, *So much excitement. I'm going to have to spend another week in bed to recover.* But he let himself enjoy a small smile as he had to admit, the party was fun.

"Hello!" said a voice. Once more, if he wasn't so exhausted, he would have jumped a mile because he thought the kitchen was empty. Slowly he turned around, but nobody was there!

"Hello?" he said.

"Hello!" said the voice, and he realised it was the cottage wall speaking to him.

"You look amazing," Mr Bowns complimented the wall, because it's a very polite thing to do.

"Thank you," said the wall. "Your friends have been brilliant, scrubbing, polishing, and mending me until I'm as good as new, if not better! I feel great! I'm so glad the witch didn't kill you and your friends."

"Me too," he agreed, just as the children came into the kitchen.

"There you are – hiding from your own party," teased Joanne. "We thought you would be in here. Have you met the cottage?"

Before he could answer, a goblin burst in through the back door. He was covered in dirt and sweat, and he stood in the doorway for a few moments getting his breath back. Everybody stared at him, barely daring to blink. Between breaths, he said, "Help... Where is the... witch?"

Everyone looked at each other, then Jake said, "She's gone. We got rid of her and now we're having a party."

"Oh no. That's not good. That is very, very, bad. Who is going to save us from the ogre if the witch has gone?"

All eyes turned to Mr Bowns, who simply sighed, slowly stood up, and mumbled to himself, "Effort, effort, effort. Come on then, lead the way."

...not the end...